Anthill Home Repair

by Patricia M. Stockland
illustrated by Ryan Haugen

visit us at
www.abdopublishing.com

Printed in the United States.

Text by Patricia M. Stockland
Illustrations by Ryan Haugen
Edited by Nadia Higgins
Interior layout and design by Becky Daum
Cover design by Becky Daum

Library of Congress Cataloging-in-Publication Data
Stockland, Patricia M.
  Anthill home repair / Patricia M. Stockland ; illustrated by Ryan Haugen.
     p. cm. — (Safari friends—Milo & Eddie)
  ISBN 978-1-60270-082-6
 [1. Elephants—Fiction. 2. Monkeys—Fiction. 3. Ants—Fiction. 4. Dwellings—Fiction. 5. Grasslands—Fiction. 6. Africa—Fiction.] I. Haugen, Ryan, 1972- ill. II. Title.
PZ7.S865Ant 2008
[E]—dc22

                    2007036991

"Home for sale. 467 bedrooms. 1 bathroom. Low, low price." Milo the monkey read the sign in front of the anthill. Then, he shook his head sadly.

"I just don't understand why the ants would want to go away," Eddie the elephant said to Milo. "It's so pleasant in this corner of the great, great grasslands. Perfect ant weather. And frankly, that's just a lot of ants to move."

Milo scratched his head. "Well, if you're so confused, why don't you ask Anastasia why they are leaving?"

Anastasia, the queen ant, was old friends with Eddie. The elephant and the ant had marched two by two at last year's grasslands parade.

"Why, that's a fantastic idea!" Eddie exclaimed. With that, he politely tapped his trunk on the front door of the anthill. "Hello? I say, helloooo . . . Is anyone home?"

"Who, who, who goes there?" asked Angus, the head worker ant, as he flung open the door.

"Well, hello there! It's Eddie and Milo," answered Eddie.

"Hmmmmmm. Responding to the ANT-vertisement, no doubt. Well, I can't say you two are going to fit in here very comfortably. But I am happy, happy, happy to show you around."

Angus swung around to head back inside. "Wait!" cried Milo. "Actually, we aren't looking for a new house. We were wondering if we could talk to her highness, Anastasia."

Angus paused in the doorway.

"Are you crazy, crazy, crazy?" Angus's antennae waved in all directions. "Her highness has 934 ants to move. She's far too busy, busy, busy."

"Oh, sorry. It's just that we wanted to know. . . ," Milo began to say.

Just then, Anastasia popped her head through the doorway. "Eddie? Is that you?" she called out. She spotted her friend. "Eddie! And is that Milo with you? Helloooo. Helloooo!"

"Yes, yes. Hello, Anastasia!" Eddie was happy to see his friend. "We saw the FOR SALE sign, and I have to say, I am so sad you are moving away. May we ask why?"

At that, Anastasia's antennae and her six legs drooped like fallen kite strings.

Angus shot his queen a worried look. "You see, see, see," he began, "the house is a mess, mess, mess."

"Yes," Anastasia sighed. She stood up a little. She pointed to the cracked foundation, the cracked walls, the cracked windows, and the crumbling chimney. "And the worst part is that the bathtub doesn't work. It makes things rather difficult for 934 ants."

Eddie and Milo looked at the messes. Yes, the home did need some help. "But Anastasia, you are our friend. We don't want you to leave," sighed Eddie.

"But, that's not all!" stated Angus. "We are surrounded by termite mounds, mounds, mounds. They all look just like our anthill! We can never, never, never find our way home!"

With that, the ant kicked the side of the house. *Crash!* The front door fell off.

"Oh, heavens to hyenas!" wailed Anastasia, bursting into tears. "Who will buy our anthill now? Whatever are we going to do?!"

"Anastasia!" Eddie exclaimed. "What if Milo and I help with your home repairs? If the anthill were repaired, would you stay?"

"How, how, how can you help?" Angus interrupted. He couldn't imagine how an elephant and a monkey could know that much about the finer points of anthill architecture.

"Well, it just so happens that we recently invented an excellent recipe for mud. It's the muddiest mud ever!" replied Eddie. "In fact, Milo used the magic mud to make his prize-winning banana statue at the grasslands county fair."

Milo grinned shyly. "Well, just second prize, really, no big deal." The monkey was blushing even through his fur.

Immediately, Eddie started digging a new mini-watering hole next to the anthill. Milo joined him, and soon, the pair was mixing a gloppy slop of mud.

"We've come across some wonderful ingredients right here on the savanna!" Eddie explained. "We mix bananas, banana peels, peanut shells, water, savanna dirt, and some great, great grass! And then we add just a dash of Natural Shine Zebra Coat Polish, for extra sticking power."

Angus inspected the new building materials. "This is amazing mud, mud, mud!"

Milo admired the shimmering mud, and soon he was inspired. "Aha!" he said, bouncing up as much as he could with his super sticky feet.

"I just might have a solution to your termite problem," the monkey said. He filled a giant banana-leaf sac with mud. "I'm off to work," he said rather mysteriously. And off he went with his bag of mud behind a stand of bushes.

"I do believe we're ready for home repairs," declared Eddie. He began caking mud all about the anthill, around, over, under, and around again. Mud flew everywhere.

"I'm singin' in the mud, just singin' in the mud," Eddie sang, as he pulled a pipe out from the side of the anthill.

Angus raised an antenna. He wasn't sure how an elephant could fix a tiny ant bathtub with his huge, round, fingerless feet, but pretty soon the pipes were fixed!

Before Anastasia and Angus could say "orangutan," Eddie was finished. The anthill was once again radiant. The peanut shells and banana peels made a perfect plaster. The magnificent mud had worked like magic.

"Absolutely *fabulous!*" exclaimed Anastasia, clapping her antennae. "The door is back on! The foundation is fixed! The walls are wonderful! The chimney is cheerful again!"

"But wait, wait, wait a second," said Angus. "What about the termite mounds? How are we going to find our way home?"

"No problem!" Milo yelled as he came jumping out from behind the bushes. He was dragging a huge, lumpy something behind him. The mysterious object was draped with a white cloth.

"Ta-da!" Milo said as he pulled the cloth off with a quick flick of his tail.

Eddie and the ants gasped.

"Why, it's beautiful!" exclaimed Anastasia as she stared at a gigantic ant sculpture.

Milo scaled up the side of the ant's house. He placed the sculpture on the very top of the hill so it could be seen from miles away.

"We'll never lose our way, way, way again," Angus said.

"I hope that means you'll stay," Milo said.

"Oh yes, yes, yes," Anastasia replied.

"Hooray! Hooray! Hooray!" they all cheered.

Savanna Facts

Ants and termites are distantly related types of insects. Both live in social colonies that have different levels of parents, soldiers, and workers.

Termite mounds are much larger than anthills. But both structures show how well these creatures cooperate and how strong they are.

Ant colonies vary greatly in size. Some have just a few dozen members, while others can have millions of ants.